WITHDRAWN

BIG TROUBLE

Halt, adventurer, and read these words before you proceed!

You are about to embark on a journey. To where, only you could possibly say. It is not a journey like any you have been on before, where you start at page one and continue on a straight course until you reach the end. Instead you will be presented with many choices along the way. Each time you are faced with one such choice, make your decision from the options given and then follow the directions to proceed. Once your quest has come to an end, either favorably or, as I'm afraid in some instances it is foretold to, gruesomely, return to the beginning and start again.

This is not a journey for those who prefer to sit back and let others make the tricky decisions. This is a journey for a leader, a true hero. One who is not afraid to charge headlong into a lair of orcs or fight alongside giants. If this doesn't sound like you, turn back now and forget you ever came this way. But if this whiff of adventure has whet your appetite, then forward with you, my friend. And good luck!

CANDLEWICK
ENTERTAINMENT

BIG TROUBLE

MATT FORBECK

The ground of Ardeep Forest trembles, and you are troubled. It has always felt firm and stable before this.

"What's happening?" you ask as you push yourself away from your ancient desk, fashioned by magic from the living trunk of a tree far older than you. You've been studying the elven scrolls strewn across it all week, deciphering the notes and sigils scrawled upon them by wizards much wiser than you—in this case, your parents—and you were on the edge of a breakthrough in your understanding of them. That will have to wait for now.

Your younger brother lets out a large belch. "Excuse me!" He flashes you a goofy grin as he rubs his belly, entirely unaware that there might be any problem.

"Quiet, Talaren," your mother says to him as she cocks her head to one side to listen. She focuses her attention far away for a moment, then her eyes snap back to you, filled with panic. "We need to leave!" she says. "Now!"

You start to gather up your scrolls to put them away, but your mother shakes her head at you. "We don't have time for that."

Your father bursts through the front door of your cozy home, a tower built into the center of a massive hollow tree. "Trouble is coming," he says to you all. "Big trouble."

"What kind, Malaren?" your mother asks him as she gathers up her spell components, the special little odds and ends she needs to work her wizardly magic. "Did you see?"

"Does it matter, Ardenna? We have to leave, whatever kind it is."

"But why?" Talaren asks. "Isn't being safe one of the reasons we live here?"

He's right, you know. The tower-tree you call home blends in so well with the other trees in Ardeep Forest that you sometimes have trouble picking it out yourself. It's how your parents keep people from the nearby metropolis of Waterdeep from constantly knocking on your door.

"Such camouflage doesn't matter to the creatures coming this way," your father says as he puts your brother's hand in yours.

You can feel your brother trembling. If you weren't frightened before, you're starting to feel that way now.

Your father scurries about, stuffing necessary things into his pack. "They knock over everything in their path. Our home will be just another tree to them, something else to flatten."

"Who are they?" your brother asks.

You're not sure you want to hear the answer.

"Giants!" your father says as he leads you toward the front door. "People as tall as a house. Taller even than our tree! They're coming this way, and they're hungry."

He flings open the door, and you squeeze your brother's hand, ready to run as fast as you can, but before you take your first step, you see exactly what your father was talking about: a massive person stands before you, blotting out the sun.

"Hide!" your mother says to you. "Take your brother and go!"

Run! Turn to page 6 . . .
Face the giants! Turn to page 8 . . .
Hide! Turn to page 16 . . .

You gape at the kobolds in horror. "You can't be serious!" you tell them. "There's a giant coming after us, and he's going to kill us all!"

"Such lies you elves tell!" the leader of the kobolds says as he jabs his spear at you. "You can't fool us! We know thunder when we hear it!"

Under other circumstances, you might laugh at them. You stand at least a foot taller than even the largest of the scaly, snout-faced creatures. While they outnumber you and Talaren, you could probably scare them off with the little bit of magic you know. But this isn't funny at all.

As it is, you're all doomed. The kobolds have halted any chance you had of outrunning the giant—which was going to be a challenge anyhow. And you very much doubt that the giant will show them any mercy for the favor they've done it.

"You're fools! All of you!" you scream at the top of your lungs. Alarmed by your outburst, Talaren begins to wail.

If the giant wasn't exactly sure where to find you before, it knows now. It bursts through the trees and grins down at the kobolds with a wide mouth filled with rotting teeth. The pack of little creatures recoils in terror. Delighted at their reaction, the giant lays into them with a long log that it picked up and is using as a rough club.

"You did this to us!" the kobold leader cries as his people are crushed by the giant's blows. He charges straight at you as you try to flee, and he stabs you in the back with his spear.

You give him a grim smile as your life leaves you. You take small comfort in the fact that at least your killer won't survive—but maybe Talaren still has a chance.

THE END

Still holding your little brother by the hand, you run for the back door, pushing as fast and hard as you can.

"Where are we going?" Talaren shouts, scared and confused as you knock over anything in your way.

"Anywhere but here!" you tell him as you drag him through the door and into the forest beyond. You emerge into the sun-dappled shadows of the undergrowth in which you've played for your entire life. Normally, you'd find that comforting, but today the sight brings you no joy at all.

You're barely step out of the tower before you hear a massive explosion behind you, followed almost immediately by a crack of thunder that nearly leaves you deaf. Talaren freezes, frightened by the horrible noises, but you're not about to let him stop you from fleeing. You tug on his hand, but he acts as if his legs have stopped working.

You pick the boy up in your arms, and he clings to you like life's last breath. You know you can't move all that fast with him weighing you down, but it never occurs to you to leave him behind. If you're going to die, you're going to die together. After all, if you left him behind, your parents would kill you anyhow!

You stagger through the woods, Talaren in your arms, as fast as you can. You don't get a hundred feet before your home comes down behind you with a massive crash that shatters the smaller trees in its path. Splinters blast past you, flying like tiny arrows. Talaren's scream of horror pierces your ears and sets them ringing. You want to join in, but you don't have the time or the breath.

You glance over your shoulder and spy the culprit who just felled your home: an enormous hill giant that stands three times your height. It towers there in the gap the absence of your home forms in the forest, like a missing tooth torn from a mouth. It stares at you from the ruin of your home and shouts after you. "Hey, come back here!"

You know that to listen to the giant is to court death. If you followed its order, it would kill you both for sure.

You keep running instead, even though you're aware that the giant can catch up to you with just a few of its massive strides. At the very least, you're determined to not be easy prey. The darkest part of Ardeep Forest calls to you—but maybe you'd be better off leaping into the river instead?

Dive into Ardeep River! Turn to page 12...
Run deeper into the forest! Turn to page 14...

You know your parents want you to hide, to protect your little brother, but where can you go that's safe from such a monster?

"Go," you say to Talaren. "Hide!"

"I want to help!" he insists.

"No." You cast a little charm on him to get him to agree. Normally you'd never do such a thing to him, but this is life and death. "In the cellar. Go!"

You hope he'll be safe there, although if a giant decides to dig into the earth, you don't suppose there would be any stopping it.

You turn back to look for your parents, but they've already run out of your home to face the giant. Your father moves off to the left, while your mother charges to the right. You don't know which way you should go, so you stop in the doorway and look for some way you might be able to help.

The giant towers over you, standing three times your height and roaring like a storm. It seems as thick around as a tree, but you don't have those to compare the creature to anymore, as everything in a large swath behind the giant has been knocked flat, like wheat beneath a scythe.

Your father shouts magic words as he plucks something out of the pouch he wears on his belt and hurls it in the direction of the giant. As the substance reaches the creature, it suddenly explodes into a huge ball of fire that scorches your face, even as far away from it as you are. The giant rears back, roaring in pain as its blanket-length beard bursts into scorching flames.

The giant tumbles backward, knocking over another tree as it goes. The ground beneath you shakes, tossing you from your feet. As you scramble to your knees, you look up to see that the giant your father took down is not alone. There are two more!

"Go away!" your mother shouts to your right. You look over and see her rubbing a crystal rod with a bit of fur. "Leave us alone!"

She points the rod at one of the other giants, and a bolt of lightning arcs from the tip, disintegrating the rod as it goes. The electricity lances through the creature's chest, and it lets loose a screech that makes your ears feel like they're going to bleed. It crumples to its knees, and the impact knocks you flat once more.

You drag yourself forward and watch as the third giant attacks your parents. It kicks your father aside with a sweep of its leg, sending him sailing into the trees. It slaps your mother down hard, driving her into the loamy dirt of the forest floor.

You scream in protest at the giant's attack. This only serves to draw its attention to you.

The last thing you see is the bottom of the giant's boot hurtling down toward you.

THE END

There's no way you can outrun the giant on land. You realize the water's your only chance. Clutching Talaren to your chest, you charge straight toward the quick-flowing Ardeep River, and you dive straight into it.

"Hold your breath!" you say to Talaren just before you hit the water.

To his credit, your brother does as you tell him. You dive deep and stay under the river's surface as long as you can, letting the current sweep you both downstream. The water is so cold that you can't bear to be beneath it much longer. When you surface, you see the giant standing knee-deep in the river, searching the murky depths for you.

The giant turns and spots you, letting out a thunderous roar that makes the water around you quiver.

With Talaren still in your arms, you start kicking for the opposite shore, but there's no chance you'll make it there in time—not before the giant gets you.

Turn to page 15...

You refuse to give up hope. Although you seem doomed for sure, you throw back your head and shout for help. "Pleasc! Someone! Anyone! Help us!"

You don't know whom you expect to answer you. The band of little lizard-faced kobolds certainly aren't going to come to your aid. Maybe your mother or your father will hear you? Maybe the gods will answer your plea?

Instead, to your delight, one of the trees nearest you bends over and scoops you and Talaren up in its branches. Shocked, the kobolds scurry out of the way.

"Leaf and root!" the tree says to you. "What kind of trouble are you two in?"

You see then that the tree is a creature known as a treant. He's ncarly as tall as a giant, but likely not as strong.

"A giant is chasing us!" you explain, pointing in the direction from which you can hear the monster coming closer.

"Not for long!" the treant says as he strides away with you.

Soon you and Talaren are safe. Rathcr than face down the giants, the treant takes you and your brother to his grove. When your parents fail to come find you, the treant and his wife raise you as their own.

THE END

While the giant may have the advantage on you in terms of size and strength, it doesn't know Ardeep Forest the way you do. The woods have been your backyard for your entire life. If anyone can lose a giant here, it's you.

Still carrying Talaren, you weave your way deeper and deeper into the forest, cutting back and forth through valleys and over hills. The giant stays on your tail, knocking over every tree you put between you and it.

You don't know how long you can keep this up. Your legs grow tired, and your breath draws short. Just as you're about to give up and let the giant crush you, though, a strange voice shouts at you: "Halt!"

You skid to a stop and see that you're surrounded by a band of spear-wielding kobolds that don't seem to have realized the danger you're all in.

Confront the kobolds! Turn to page 4 . . .
Call for help! Turn to page 13 . . .

Talaren screeches in terror again, but this time it's not because of the giant. A humongous bird known as a roc swoops down and plucks you and your brother out of the river before the giant can reach you.

While in its claws, you realize that the creature didn't do this to save you, as it doesn't set you down until it reaches its nest—which is full of four hungry hatchlings!

Each of the young birds is bigger than you are, but rather than gulping you down whole, they set to fighting one another over which one of them gets to eat you and your brother. While they bicker, the two of you slip through the gaps in the bottom of their nest and escape!

When you reach the ground, you realize you have no idea where you are, but at least you're free of the rocs—and the giants!

THE END

You do exactly as your parents suggest and hide. There's no place inside the main part of the tower-tree that's sure to be safe, so you decide to dive into the cellar beneath it instead. It's deep enough that even if the entire place comes down, you might survive.

Still holding your little brother by the hand, you haul him toward the cellar door, but he fights you all the way.

"No!" he screams. "Mother! Father!"

"It's safer than staying up here!" you try to explain, but he continues to fight you.

You don't blame him for wanting to help your parents, as foolish as that would be. You have the same urge yourself. But the roar of the giants outside sounds like the approach of a hurricane, and while he might be too young to understand, you know neither of you can stand against them.

You hear an explosion outside, followed by a crack of thunder so close you're astonished that the lightning didn't split open the tree. You make the mistake of covering your ears against the noise as you pull open the hatch for the cellar, and that's what allows Talaren to squirm free from your grasp.

The boy spins on his heels and charges back toward the tower's front door. "Mother!" he shouts. "Father! Hold on, I'm coming!"

You leap up from the cellar hatch to sprint after him, but that's when the tree starts to come apart all around you. It begins with a loud thump as something hits the outside of it, causing the entire place to shake as if an earthquake has hit it. Then the tree cracks open near the bottom, and light begins streaming in.

You cast about for Talaren, hoping you can save him—or at least be with him when the end comes—but you can't find him anywhere. You dash toward the front door, hoping to spot him again, and there he is, reaching for the door.

"Mother! Father!" he calls again.

"No, Talaren!" you shout. He doesn't seem to hear you at all. "Come back!"

Suddenly, as the tower-tree rumbles around you, Talaren hauls up short and glances back at you. At that moment, you can see in his eyes that he's sorry. He knows what he did was wrong and that it put both your lives in danger.

But he just can't help it. He loves your parents too much to ever leave them.

He swallows hard and opens his mouth to say something to you, but the words don't come out.

An instant later, an entire wall of the tower-tree disappears as a giant knocks it down with a blow from an enormous club, exposing you and Talaren to its rage. The force of its roar knocks you backward through the hatch and into the cellar. You hit your head on the stairs as you go, and blackness takes you.

You awaken sometime later and emerge from the

ruins of your home. Talaren is gone, as are your mother and father. You have no idea where they've disappeared to — or even if they're still alive. You've never felt so alone in your entire life.

You shade your eyes to look up into the sky, and you spot something that steals your breath away: a gigantic tower hovering in the air above where your tower-tree once stood. This one is made of stone rather than wood, but despite that, it defies gravity's pull.

A massive ladder leads down from the front of the floating tower, and a cloud giant stands in front of it, looking at you. This one's even bigger than the ones who destroyed your home, almost five times your height, but he seems more restrained. He has gray hair and a long, well-kept beard, and he wears a wizard's robes. He gazes at you with a wide, relieved smile.

"Thank Memnor you're not dead," he rumbles. "I'm Zephyros, a friend of your parents'. I heard about the hill giant invasion, and I came to defend against it." He surveys the ruins. "It seems I'm too late, but perhaps I can help."

After weighing his options, Zephyros takes you in his flying tower to visit Claugiyliamatar, an ancient green dragon that lives in nearby Kryptgarden Forest. "If there were any other choice . . ." he says.

"I hate the hill giants," the dragon tells you when you arrive, "and the feeling is mutual." She licks her lips as she says this, though, and you wonder if she might find you tasty.

She consults her large collection of crystal balls to see

if she can figure out what happened to your parents. As she does, she gasps with delight. "I found them both! Your father, it seems, is traveling north to the Eye of the All-Father, faster than you could believe, while your mother, along with your brother, is being taken to Grudd Haug, a hill giant settlement to the south."

Zephyros looks down at you, eager to leave. "Which way would you like to go?"

Follow your mother's path. Turn to page 25 . . .
Follow your father's path. Turn to page 26 . . .

You probably should have called for Harshnag, who can't see you this far down the passageway, at least not from where you left him, but you're tired of relying on giants to do everything for you. You want to handle these attacking barbarians yourself.

You are a fool. You try to cast a spell to stop them, but the barbarians don't even give you a chance to let the words leave your lips. They knock you to the stone floor, crushing the breath from your lungs. Before you know it, you have a gag in your mouth and your hands are bound behind you. Someone puts a rough sack over your head and throws you over a well-muscled shoulder.

You try to scream, but it's no use. You hope the barbarians might do something to tip off Harshnag, but they manage to steal out of the temple complex without him noticing they have you.

You travel with them for a full day before they rip the hood off your head. You find yourself in a longhouse, sitting before a raging fire, the feeling finally flowing back into your fingers and toes. A woman draped in furs and beads sits before you and says, "Welcome. I am Retgut and you will be my apprentice."

Turn to page 81...

As Zephyros's flying tower comes to a hovering stop over the fight raging in the middle of the snow-capped mountains, the battle between the two frost giants reaches a crescendo. One of them swings his battle-ax at the other and knocks his foe backward to the edge of a cliff. The injured giant hangs there for a moment, windmilling his arms as he struggles to fight his momentum, before he topples into the abyss below.

You gasp in horror as the victorious giant throws back his head and bellows in triumph.

Zephyros tries to comfort you. "That's Harshnag below us," he says. "Fortunately, he won."

Zephyros puts you on his shoulder, where you sit perched like a bird as he climbs down the ladder from his flying tower. By the time he sets foot on the mountain, Harshnag stands there ready for him, his gigantic battle-ax holstered at his waist.

"What do you want, wizard?" the frost giant says with a suspicious glare.

Zephyros gestures toward you and explains. "This is the child of Malaren and Ardenna, friends of mine from Ardeep Forest who have gone missing. We believe Malaren seeks the Eye of the All-Father so that he can find his wife, and this little one would like to find him."

Harshnag tugs at his beard as he considers the request. Soon he comes to a decision and addresses you directly.

"I can take you to the Eye, but it's a threatening journey to an even more dangerous place. I will be happy to

help you on this hazardous quest if that's what you're set on. But if you're not up to such a harrowing undertaking, you can remain with your wizard friend here while I go search for your father myself."

Stay with Zephyros. Turn to page 31 . . .
Go with Harshnag. Turn to page 40 . . .

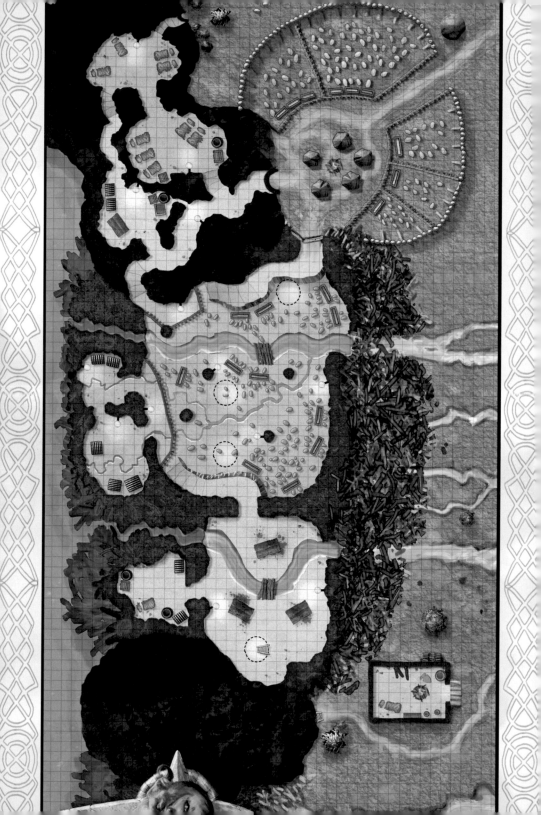

If my father's alive, I'm sure he'll be all right on his own," you tell Zephyros. "I think I should go after my mother and brother instead. They'll need me more."

The cloud giant harrumphs. "Then let's get going."

You return with Zephyros to his flying tower and immediately head south. As you travel, Zephyros shows you the location of Grudd Haug on a map.

"It's not that far from Ardeep Forest," he says.

"But why would they attack us?" you ask. "We've never had any sort of trouble like this before."

"There are strange things happening among the giants these days," Zephyros says. "Many jockey for favor among our gods, and some don't care who gets hurt in the process."

"That's why they destroyed our home?"

Zephyros gives you a grim frown. "The leader of this particular group of hill giants is a female named Guh. She believes that the bigger and fatter she gets, the more the gods will favor her. She's sent her people out into the world to forage for her."

You grimace. "And she has my mother and brother?"

"For now." Zephyros tries to comfort you. "If they're not already dead, she must be keeping them for some purpose. We haven't run out of time yet."

He lands his tower just out of sight of Grudd Haug. "I can't stay, I'm afraid. I don't get involved in giant politics," he explains. "But I wish you the greatest luck."

Turn to page 28 . . .

I need to find my father," you say as Zephyros escorts you safely from the lair of the green dragon and back to his flying tower. "But what is the Eye of the All-Father?"

"It's a temple dedicated to Annam the All-Father, the leader of the giant gods," Zephyros explains as he lifts you into his tower. "We giants know it as an oracle that can help us divine the threats that face us in the world. I suspect your father became separated from your mother in the battle with the hill giants. He must have gone there to discover what happened to her."

"How do we get there?" you ask hopefully as Zephyros climbs up into the tower after you.

"It lies hidden under the Spine of the World, a mountain chain far to the north. I don't know how to find it myself—its location is a tightly kept secret—but I know someone who does. His name is Harshnag, a frost giant who fancies himself something of an adventurer."

"He doesn't sound easy to find either," you say.

Zephyros chuckles at this. "It's far simpler to find him than the Eye of the All-Father. Harshnag doesn't avoid attention. You might instead say that he likes to court it. Once we reach the Spine of the World, we should be able to locate him in no time."

You're not sure if you believe Zephyros, but if you want to find your father, you don't have much choice.

The tower flies to the north, and days later, you begin to scour a snow-capped chain of mountains, hunting for this giant adventurer.

The thunderous noise of a battle between two frost giants draws you to Harshnag.

"There he is!" Zephyros says as he brings the flying tower in closer to the hard-fought clash.

Turn to page 22 . . .

Y ou would complain to Zephyros for not coming with you for the most crucial part of your mission, but he's already done so much for you. Instead, you bid him good-bye, praying that one day you might see him again, and march in the direction of Grudd Haug.

Your legs quake beneath you with every step, and you hope that you look more confident than you feel. From the map Zephyros showed you, you know that Grudd Haug lies to the northeast of Ardeep Forest along a branch of the Dessarin River, which also runs past northern Ardeep before reaching Waterdeep and tumbling into the Sea of Swords.

A number of times you are forced to hide in the undergrowth as all manner of unsightly beings pass you on the path. One time you think you have been spotted by an especially slow goblin who has fallen behind the rest of the pack, but he pauses only long enough to glance slyly around him and shove an apple into his mouth from the loaded basket he carries.

You smell Grudd Haug before you see it, and the stench nearly makes you gag. As you crest a hill, you finally spy it. It straddles the Dessarin like a gigantic beaver dam, letting the water trickle past to the west. The base of the structure seems to be made of massive logs stacked together and stuck to one another with muddy clay. A long hall is fashioned from timber and dried mud, roofed over by long logs packed with mud and thatch.

Giants, goblins, hobgoblins, and ogres stream in and out of the hall, and you know that if you want to find your mother and brother, you're going to have to somehow get inside.

Sneak in. Turn to page 113...
Charge in! Turn to page 33...
Disguise yourself. Turn to page 78...

You find a leash next to the pigpen and put it on one of the pigs. Then you haul the squealing animal out of the pen and toward the main hall. The pig fights you the entire way, and many of the goblins nearby laugh at your efforts. None of them offer to help.

When you enter the hall, you spot Guh sitting atop a cart that she's crushed under her weight. She's massive, even for a hill giant. She sits among thick rolls of fat that seem to curl in on one another, and you wonder how she can manage to breathe under so much excess weight.

The pig squeals even louder as you draw closer to Guh. As you go, you spot your mother and brother in a cage off to your right. Unable to recognize you through your disguise, they shy away from your horrible task.

Feed Guh the pig. Turn to page 50...
Try to free your family. Turn to page 54...

You see the wisdom in accepting Harshnag's offer to look for your father while you stay with Zephyros, and you decide to remain in the safety of the tower. Zephyros takes his home high into the air over the Spine of the World, and you stay there for a week before you realize that Harshnag isn't coming back.

"Is he dead?" you ask Zephyros, worried that you sent the giant hero to an ill fate.

"I've seen him survive much worse," Zephyros says. "We will continue to look for him. Meanwhile, you are welcome to stay with me for as long as you like."

Many years pass, but you find no trace of your family, nor of Harshnag. Eventually you give them all up for dead. You've become comfortable in Zephyros's tower, though, and continue on there as his apprentice. He teaches you far more about magic than your parents ever could have, and you vow to one day avenge their deaths.

Just not today.

THE END

After coming all this way, you don't see the point in sneaking around. You rush straight down to Grudd Haug and charge in.

At least that's your plan. You're only halfway down the hill that leads to Grudd Haug before a goblin guard spots you and sounds the alarm. You freeze for a moment, unsure of what you should do. When five full-size hill giants emerge from the main hall and charge after you though, you realize that you've made a terrible mistake.

You spin on your heels and flee. Unfortunately, while the hill giants aren't very smart or terribly quick, their legs are much longer than yours. "Gonna get you!" they shout. "You're mine!"

They catch up to you long before you make it to the top of the hill.

The first of the giants to reach you stoops to pick you up. "No!" the others say. "It's mine! Mine! Mine! Mine!"

They start shoving one another around, especially the giant that's holding you. He clutches you close to his chest to keep the others from taking you away. That works until he trips and falls over on top of you.

THE END

As you peer around the room from the safety of darkness, you spy a cage set into one corner of the main hall. Your mother and brother are inside it!

A goblin has a spear pressed against your brother's neck, forcing your mother to cast a spell.

"Hurry up, elf!" the goblin says. "Chief Guh is hungry."

In a flash of light, a feast's worth of food appears on a blanket spread before them.

A handful of goblins scurry forward to collect the food and throw it into a wheelbarrow. Then they roll the wheelbarrow up a wooden ramp they've constructed that leads right up to Guh's mouth. Once there, they upend the wheelbarrow, dumping all of the food into the giant's massive maw. The sight turns your stomach.

You look back at your mother and see that she's exhausted. She's a great wizard, but they must be forcing her to expend all her energy keeping Guh fed. You shudder to think what they might do to her and your brother once they have no further use for them.

Go to your family. Turn to page 38 . . .
Approach Guh. Turn to page 45 . . .

You slide off the slope and into the open air, plummeting toward seemingly certain death. Instead, you wind up caught in a frost-rimmed web that bounces like a net as it catches you well short of the bottom of the chasm into which you've fallen.

You sigh with relief for a moment, but when you try to move, you realize that you're stuck firmly in the web. You struggle against it until your strength gives out, but you're unable to free yourself from its sticky strands.

You lie there trapped in the web for hours. The battle with the dragon ends, but if your father and Harshnag wound up on the winning side, they don't seem to be able to figure out where you went. You ran and hid a bit too well.

You start shouting for help, but none comes. You worry that you might be guiding the dragon to you, but at this point that seems better than dying of thirst while you're stuck in this web.

At night, the temperature plunges, and you understand that you're going to freeze to death long before you can succumb to thirst. You can't stop shivering.

When the ice spiders finally come for you, you close your eyes and wait for their poisonous bites.

THE END

You cast your spell, and a portion of the mound of bones and other refuse beneath Guh begins to slide toward the cooking fire near the center of the room. Once the grotesquely rotund giant begins slipping in that direction, there seems to be no stopping her. The oils that have accumulated on her skin—both from herself and from the things that she's eaten—help accelerate her slide.

The bulbous giant screams in terror as she realizes that she's lost control of herself. She reaches out with her arms to try to slow her movement, but her hands are covered in grease from the fatty foods she likes to eat. Her fingers cannot find purchase.

She gains speed as she slides forward. "Help me!" she calls out to the followers that surround her, but no one is willing to risk being crushed under her enormous bulk.

Guh flails about, trying to stop herself but failing miserably. She's moving at a good clip by the time she smashes into the cooking fire. As she does so, she knocks over the iron tripod suspending a giant kettle over the fire, and the kettle tumbles down into the coals, which burst into a great hissing ball of steam.

Guh screams in agony, burned by the fire and scalded by the steam. The billowing steam expands throughout the room almost instantly, filling it not only with sweltering heat but with the stench of burning flesh.

You run down the ramp that led up to Guh's face and sprint over to the cage in which your mother and brother are being held. You call to them quietly, not wanting to alert any of the giants or their compatriots that you're trying to break your family out of their prison, but you get no answer. You rattle the door and find that it's loose. You enter, but there's nobody there.

You're not sure where they've gone, but you know you don't want to be caught in the cage when the steam and smoke clear. You stumble blindly out of the cage and through the hall until you emerge from the building, which now seems to be ablaze.

You slip away into the darkness and immediately spot your mother and brother! They've been waiting there for you, unwilling to leave the area without you. After the three of you silently celebrate your reunion, you lead them up and over the hill and disappear with them into the night.

"What about Father?" Talaren asks as you head toward your destroyed tower.

"He's looking for us," you tell him. "Hopefully he makes the right choices that will bring him back home too."

Your father doesn't return, but your mother often tells you how proud he would be of you. When you're old enough, you become an adventurer so you can see the world—and maybe find him. From time to time you hear tales of an elf fighting with giants, and although the tales don't lead you back to your father, you never give up hope.

THE END

You bide your time, and when no one is looking—mostly because Guh seems like she might throw up at that point—you slip over the windowsill and into the main hall. You duck down low and hold your breath for a moment, waiting for someone to point at you and raise an alarm. When no one does, you breathe a silent sigh of relief and force yourself to move.

You stick to the shadows along the wall and work your way to the cage where your mother and brother are resting. There's a pile of hay next to the cage, and you crawl through it until you're close enough to speak with them without (you hope) anyone else hearing you.

"Mother!" you whisper. "Talaren!"

Their ears perk up at the sound of your voice, and they glance around, looking for you. When they finally realize where you're hiding—they can see your face emerging from the side of the haystack—it's all your mother can do to keep your brother from shouting out in joy.

"What can I do to get you out of here?" you ask your mother as quietly as you can.

"Leave us!" she says, her eyes filled with fear for your safety as she slowly removes her hand from where she had it clamped over Talaren's mouth. "Come back for us once you find your father!"

"He's gone north to search for you," you explain. "He'll never get back here in time."

"Then we're doomed," Talaren says as tears begin to roll down his cheeks. "Doomed . . ."

Your mother clutches him to her and whispers comforting words into his ear. You wish she could do the same for you, but you're the only hope either one of them has left.

Somewhere behind you, there's a horrible retching sound followed by a massive splash. An odor reaches your nose soon after that makes you feel even more sick to your stomach.

You realize that Guh has just made more room in her belly for her next meal.

"Still hungry!" Guh hollers from the other side of the hall. "Feed me! More!"

"Coming right up!" someone shouts at her. "Hurry, you dogs! Feed the chief! Now!"

A shadow falls over you, and you look up to see a hill giant glaring down at you. "What's this, then?" he demands.

You yelp in protest and dive deep into the hay, but it's no use. The giant reaches in and scatters the hay about, exposing you in no time flat. Then he grabs you by one of your legs and holds you in front of him, upside down. Your mother and brother scream in terror, but there's nothing they can do.

Turn to page 44 . . .

I appreciate the offer to look for my father for me," you tell Harshnag, "but this is my quest. I can't abandon it."

"Fair enough, little one," Harshnag says with a game look in his massive eyes. "Then you and I will find the Eye of the All-Father together!"

"I thought you already knew where it was," Zephyros says as he sets you down on the mountain next to the burly and eager frost giant. At least the cloud giant isn't so eager to be rid of you that he'd hand you over to someone without any sort of a plan.

"Of course I do!" Harshnag says with a sheepish yet confident grin. "It's just not always that easy to get to, if you know what I mean. That's one of the ways it's kept safe from intruders."

"It's all right," you tell Zephyros in an effort to allay his fears. While Harshnag might not seem like the most solid of allies, you have no other choice in the matter at the moment—not if you want to find your father. As tempting as it might be, you can't just hide in the cloud giant's flying tower forever.

You glance up at Harshnag, who's almost four times as tall as you—but still shorter than the cloud giant wizard. He arches an eyebrow in what you're sure he thinks is a daring manner. You'd like to be more comforted by that than you are, but you decide that it'll have to be good enough. "I think I'm in good hands."

Zephyros grumbles a bit. "I wouldn't leave you with him if I didn't agree. And I'm afraid I have pressing business elsewhere." He gives Harshnag a hard look. "You take good care of this child, though, or I'll hear about it."

"Of course," Harshnag says with an easy smile. "I always look after little ones as if they were my own." He winces for an instant at some kind of memory. "Actually, better than that."

"See that you do," says Zephyros.

You run up and hug his knees, and he gives you a gentle pat on the back.

"You take care of yourself," he says to you. "I expect to be regaled by legends about you in good time."

You can't help but laugh at that. Then he disengages from you and climbs up the ladder into his flying tower. A moment later, the tower begins floating away, and soon it's lost in the snow-choked sky.

"Let's be off!" Harshnag says once Zephyros is gone for sure. "I'd carry you, but I find that sort of extra weight throws me off in battle—and I'm always ready for a fight!"

You're disappointed that you'll have to walk, but you're not sure you want to be clinging to the giant when he gets into a battle anyhow.

He has you take the lead while he guides from behind. "Giants leave big footprints," he explains. "Don't want you stumbling in one of them."

You hike for days, and eventually you reach the place that the giant claims is where the Eye of the All-Father sits, high in a range of snow-capped mountains. Harshnag leads you through a complicated series of icy tunnels and

treacherous passages until you finally approach the entrance to the temple — at which point he stops and encourages you to enter on your own.

"They don't always like me too much in there," he says with a grimace. "And I don't want to overstay my welcome. If you need me, though, just shout for me, and I'll be there in an instant."

You reluctantly agree to this, and you proceed alone down a high, wide causeway that leads into the temple complex. You reach a vaulted dome held up by pillars, onto which have been carved life-size scenes depicting the six kinds of giants: hill, frost, cloud, storm, stone, and fire.

There's a hallway in the back of the dome that's tall enough for even the largest giant to pass through, and wider than your home. You head down it.

You don't get ten feet along the passageway before a band of barbarians leaps out of the shadows and attacks you!

Fight them! Turn to page 21 . . .
Call Harshnag for help! Turn to page 49 . . .

W ell, well, well," the giant says as he stares at you with a vicious grin on his face. "Here's a pretty little treat."

"Let me go!" you shout at him.

"Oh, I intend to," he says. "But probably not where you want me to."

"Stop!" your mother says. "Don't hurt my child!"

The giant chortles at her. "If you had any spells left, you would have already used them."

Your mother slumps forward and grabs at the bars of her cage. "If you harm a hair on my child's head—"

"I won't be harming nothing," the giant says as he carries you away, over toward Guh. "But I can't speak for the chief."

"That looks like a tasty morsel," Guh says through blubbery lips. "Gimme!"

The giant holding you is careful not to get too close to Guh himself. Instead, he tosses you up in a high arc that comes down right into the massive chief's maw.

THE END

Waiting until Guh lets loose a belch loud enough to shake the rafters of the main hall, you slip over the windowsill and hide in the shadows. You peer at your mother and brother and wish you could just walk up and let them loose, but you know that this would only bring all the giants down on you at once. If you couldn't get away from a few of them before—when you were in Ardeep Forest—you're sure that you can't manage it among so many of them here.

You work your way along the shadows toward Guh instead, and the closer you get, the more disgusted you feel. She smells like a trash heap left out in the sun for months, and you can see that the floor of the hall around her is covered with grease that's dripped off of her.

"Feed me!" Guh shouts to anyone within earshot. "Feed me so that I can become the biggest giant of them all! Then our gods will have to show me their favor!"

To you this sounds like madness — or at least just an excuse for Guh to indulge in horrific amounts of gluttony. If it weren't for the fact that her giants destroyed your home and captured your mother and brother in pursuit of her goal, you'd probably laugh at it.

Instead, you decide that there's no other way you're going to be able to free your family: you're going to have to confront Guh.

When there's a short break in the feeding, you dash onto a wooden ramp that leads up to Guh's face so that the goblins can dump food into her maw. Once you reach the top of it, you present yourself to her.

"Oh great and powerful Chief Guh!" you say. "I beg an audience with you!"

The other giants in the room gasp in horror as Guh shifts about as best she can and tries to focus her greasy eyes on you.

"Who dares interrupt my feeding?" she shouts.

"I am but a little elf from Ardeep Forest," you explain. "Your people kidnapped my mother and brother, and I'm here to ask that you set them free."

The massive pile of fat chortles at you. "And why would I do something like that? Your mother's spells have done more to keep me fed than any farm we've raided. Until the gods show me their favor, she's stuck filling my belly as fast as she can!"

She peers at you as if she's seeing you for the first time. "Now, go join your mother in her cage, or you can join my latest meal in my gullet!"

Demand that Guh free your family! Turn to page 57...
Trick Guh with magic! Turn to page 62...
Attack Guh with magic! Turn to page 86...

As soon as the barbarians emerge from the darkness, you scream for help at the top of your lungs. You're embarrassed that you need assistance already, but you don't care. You know when you're outnumbered, and you haven't come all the way to the Eye of the All-Father to die before you even manage to enter the place.

Harshnag comes roaring into the entryway and most of the barbarians scatter, fleeing for their lives. Their chief, though—a large man who still isn't even a third of Harshnag's height—shouts out "Have at thee!" and then charges at the giant.

Harshnag laughs at the man and backhands him with the flat of his battle-ax. The barbarian chief goes flying and lands in a heap at the end of the tunnel.

"I admire your pluck!" Harshnag says as he steps over the barbarian's unconscious form. "But that only goes so far in quelling my wrath!"

As you leave the fallen man behind, the rest of the barbarians scurry out of the darkness to recover their chief. Two of them throw the man's arms across their shoulders, and they scramble away as fast as they can. Harshnag's laughter haunts them as they go.

Turn to page 82 . . .

You haul the pig over to Guh, and she picks it up and shoves it into her massive maw with a single move. She swallows it down without even bothering to chew it with her rotten teeth.

A moment later, she starts to choke and turn blue. You step back, but a giant comes up from behind and grabs you, making sure you don't get away.

"What did you do?" he asks you in horror.

In your panic, you let your illusion drop, revealing your real self. The giant gasps and hauls you over to the cage holding your mother and brother. As he locks you up with them, Guh breathes her last.

Unfortunately, the other giants aren't as happy about Guh's demise as you are. Despite how much she abused them, they actually cared about her. They put your mother, brother, and you to death!

THE END

You start to laugh at your mother's defiance, but worry that this might expose you for who you really are, so you turn it into a cough instead. You get right up against the bars of the cage, hoping that you might be able to whisper a message to her. Unfrightened, she stands up to you.

You open your mouth to speak, but before you can utter a word, your mother grabs you by the throat and swings you around so that your back is against the cage. You feel a makeshift knife press against your throat, and you begin to squeal in protest.

"Back off!" your mother shouts at the other guards. "You threaten us at all, and I'll cut this one open!"

The guards each take a step back, worried that your mother is going to kill one of their kind. As they do, though, they start to take a closer look at you.

"Hold on," a hobgoblin says as he approaches from where Guh sits. "Don't do anything hasty."

A goblin sidles up next to him and points at you. "I don't know this one. Ain't from around here."

The hobgoblin squints at you suspiciously. "What's this all about, then? Who are you?"

You fall forward as you let your illusion lapse, revealing your true identity. Your mother gasps in surprise and then in dismay as she realizes whom she took hostage.

"Another elf?" the hobgoblin says with a dark chuckle. "Toss this one in to rot with the rest of them!"

A pair of goblins grab you while a handful of others keep your mother and brother at bay with spears. "And hand over that knife!" the hobgoblin says. "Or I'll feed this one to Guh right now!"

Your mother surrenders her weapon, and the goblins hurl you into the cage and slam the door behind you. Your

mother and brother gather you into their arms, and you all sob about your fate.

"How did you get here?" your mother asks.

"Where is Father?" Talaren wants to know.

"A cloud giant named Zephyros brought me here," you tell them, "but he's gone now. We learned that Father went far north to consult with something called the Eye of the All-Father to find us. As far as I know, he's still alive."

"That's wonderful!" Talaren says. A moment later, more somber, he asks, "Do you think he'll get to us in time?"

You don't know the answer to that. Unfortunately, even if your father survives his trip up north, by the time he manages to get to Grudd Haug, all he could do is avenge your deaths.

THE END

You let the pig loose, and someone else grabs it to bring it to Chief Guh. Meanwhile, you go over to the cage where your mother and brother are being held and snarl at them.

They're scared and weakened. Your brother cowers in the far corner of the cage, but your mother does not flinch at the sight of a hobgoblin come to hassle her.

You want to reach out to your mother and give her a hug, but you know the goblins guarding the cage are watching you. Instead, you growl at her and say, "You been here too long! Soon Guh will want to eat you!"

You don't know if this is true, but it gives voice to your worst fear. Your mother doesn't tremble at the thought though. Instead, she stands against the bars and says, "I hope she chokes on me!"

Turn to page 51...

Guh vomits up a river of filth. Part of this includes a pig that squeals in surprise at still being alive.

While the other giants, goblins, and hobgoblins rush up to try to help their awfully ill leader, you sprint back down the feeding ramp and head right for the cage holding your mother and brother. Your mother points toward a set of keys, which you retrieve in a flash and use to unlock the door.

The stench from the vomit is so bad that most of the others in the main hall have begun getting sick too. Even Talaren has succumbed, although you've managed to keep your dinner down so far.

You grab your brother by the hand and lead him and your mother toward freedom. Before you leave, though, you make a quick run through the shallowest part of the river so you can clean your brother off. With that chore done, you charge into the open lands beyond and hope that somehow, someday, you can leave that horrible stench behind.

"Did you have to rescue us like that?" Talaren asks.

You tousle his hair. "I didn't see any other choice!"

When you get home, you hope that your father might be waiting for you there, but he isn't. Your mother raises the two of you alone, and you become great wizards, ready to defend the land against the giants.

THE END

Y ou really think that I came all this way and walked up this ramp to confront you on my own?" you say to Guh. "My father and his friend—the mighty and powerful cloud giant wizard Zephyros—sent me ahead to parlay with you and see if we could settle this problem peacefully."

You're lying through your teeth, of course. Your only hope is that the gigantic hill giant chief isn't a good judge of character and doesn't see right through you.

She doesn't seem to care much about the threat of your father, but she recognizes the other name.

"Zephyros? Here?" She glances about the main hall as if the cloud giant might stride in at any moment and drive a massive sword through her fat-cushioned heart. She shudders so hard, the rolls of fat on her body actually quiver.

"He's coming," you tell her as sincerely as you possibly can. "And he won't be happy when he sees how you've treated his friends!"

The other giants shoot one another scared looks. Apparently Zephyros's reputation extends far among the giants. You just wish that the cloud giant had actually come with you so you wouldn't have to bluff about it. That would have made things so much easier.

"What do you mean?" Guh says in an innocent tone, waving toward the cage in which she's keeping your mother and brother. "We haven't done them any harm! I've kept them in there to protect them! Do you know how easy it is for a giant to accidentally hurt a little one? We lose all sorts of guests that way!"

"That's the flimsiest excuse I've ever heard," you tell her. "The only way Zephyros is going to accept that sort of half-hearted reasoning is if you give me a show of good faith by releasing your two guests into my custody immediately."

Guh and the rest of the giants give you blank looks. You realize you've used words with too many syllables for them to understand. You stab your finger at the ground for emphasis and shout, "Your stories won't fool a wizard. Give those people to me if you want to live! That means *now*!"

"You heard the little one!" Guh shouts at the other giants. "Release our guests! Now!"

The male hill giants turn to the goblins and hobgoblins to do the actual work of releasing your mother and brother. "Hurry!" they clamor at them. "Now!"

A few of the goblins give you hard glances, and you can tell that they don't buy into your bluff for even a dull second. You worry that they might blow it all for you.

When they see you watching them, though, they flash you wicked smiles. They might not believe in you, but they think it's hilarious to see someone — anyone, really — pulling a fast one on Guh. The goblins might be evil, but even they don't like being bossed around and ordered to do horrible things. Apparently feeding people directly into the mouth of a ravenous giant crosses the line, even for them.

Soon enough, your mother and brother are standing on shaky legs at the main hall's exit. Your mother waves for you to come down and join them, but you can't go quite yet.

"That's a good start," you tell Guh, "but we're going to need a pair of horses to ride out of here as well."

"Of course!" Guh says reluctantly. "Anything for our honored guests. Just tell Zephyros that we treated them well. There's no need for him to come here to thank us!"

"Of course not," you say as you escort your mother and brother to your steeds. "For now . . ."

As you ride out of Grudd Haug and back toward your home, you wonder if fate might be kind to your father as well. But you never see him again.

THE END

You step into the center of the circle and, with a nod from your father, ask the question that you need answered most. You don't want to waste your only chance at this, and you speak each and every word as clearly as you can, enunciating each syllable.

"Are my mother and brother still alive?"

You steel yourself for the worst. You worry that you've wasted your one question for the oracle merely to confirm what you already fear: that your mother and brother have been killed in the time it has taken you to find your father. Then you wonder if the oracle is going to bother to respond to you at all.

A moment later, a rumbling voice that seems to emanate from the walls of the gigantic chamber itself answers you.

"They are alive, although not well. The hill giant tribe working under Chief Guh has captured them both. They are keeping them in a place known as Grudd Haug."

"How long do they have?" you ask, desperate for more answers. "What can we do to help them?"

For these questions, though, the only answers are the echoes of your own voice. The oracle remains silent. You scream in frustration at the being—whoever or whatever it might be—but your father puts his hands on your shoulders to calm you down and offer you some comfort. You spin around toward him.

"We have to find Grudd Haug!" you tell him as tears well up in your eyes. "We have to save them!"

"Your mother is a capable wizard," your father tells you. "If she's with your brother, then he's in good hands."

You wipe your face dry. "We can't leave them there!"

"I know this place." Harshnag puts a hand on your father's shoulder, and you both turn to look up at him. He grimaces as he looms above you both. "Grudd Haug is a long way from here. South even of the forest from which you hail. By the time you get there, their fate will most likely already be sealed."

"That doesn't mean we shouldn't try!"

"Of course not," your father says as he escorts you from the oracle's chamber and back through the Eye of the All-Father. "We would never abandon your mother and brother, especially not when they're in such dire straits. No matter what might happen, we're going to get there as fast as we can."

"But first we have to get out of here," Harshnag says as you emerge from the complex into the windswept and snowy landscape.

Turn to page 89 . . .

I wouldn't be so hasty about making such demands!" you tell Guh as you begin to work a spell.

She seems so weak-eyed that she can't tell what you're doing, and it makes her nervous. That's good. You want her nervous.

"What are you doing?" she says. Her fat lips shiver like rubbery sausages. "Stop that. I give the orders here!"

You give her a defiant laugh, and she winces at your bravery. Evidently, it's been a long time since anyone here managed to stand up to her.

"No one laughs at me," she says, a note of uncertainty creeping into her voice. "No one!" You ignore her claims and continue with your work. Somewhere behind you, you hear a goblin softly snickering.

As you complete the spell, you glare up at Guh, defiant. "Did you really think you could lie like that forever? After all, how many giants did you have to kill to establish your power here? Did you honestly think every one of them would go quietly into the night?"

You finish your spell with a flourish of your fingers, and it conjures up the illusion of an enormous ghost that emerges from the hall's dirt floor and floats up to hover right over Guh. It is a transparent image of a female giant with long wet hair tangled with seaweed, her face and limbs waterlogged and bloated. The silent image of the dripping, dead giant reaches for the morbidly obese Guh as if it wants to tear her spirit from her body.

"No!" Guh screams as she flinches away and gapes in

utter horror. "Get her away! I didn't want to kill her! I didn't want to kill anybody!"

"But you did!" you tell her. "How many people have died to satisfy your hunger? How many more died because you desired power?"

Guh cowers before the ghostly image, looking like she wishes the mound of earth below her would swallow her whole. "I don't know! I lost count! I was just hungry! I'm always so hungry!"

The ghost dips toward the giant, but you're careful not to let it get too close. You don't want to shatter the illusion, after all. Fortunately, Guh cringes even farther away from it rather than trying to strike out.

"The spirits of the dead don't care for your excuses!" you tell her. "There's no way for someone as horrible as you to make amends!"

Guh looks to the other giants. "Help me!" she cries. "I didn't do anything wrong! I just wanted the gods to recognize my terrible beauty! What's so bad about that?"

The other giants edge away from her, unwilling to back up her claims, at least not in the presence of the angry dead. They, after all, have seen what she did.

Turn to page 68 . . .

You step into the center of the circle. It's too late to help your mother and brother. If they're still alive, they're sure to find their way back to your home one way or another. Assuming they do, you need to make sure that you all have a safe place to return to with no ongoing threat.

You announce your question clearly and carefully, making sure that the oracle can't possibly mishear you.

"What can we do to stop the giants from destroying Ardeep Forest?"

The silence that follows your question lasts for so long that you start to wonder whether the oracle actually knows the answer—maybe it's not much of an oracle after all. You're about to repeat your question, but your father lays a hand on your shoulder to give you pause, and you wait.

A moment later, a rumbling voice answers you.

"You cannot do so yourself. You don't have the power needed to accomplish such a thing."

Your heart sinks, and you wonder how the oracle could be so useless. You already know that you can't stand against the giants. Even with Harshnag and your father at your side, you would be outnumbered and overwhelmed. You open your mouth to voice your complaint, but the oracle continues.

"However, there is one who could put an end to the giants' threat. Find Elminster. He will show you the way."

The answer confuses you more than it helps. You turn to your father in despair that you've wasted your question, but he gives you a knowing smile.

"Elminster is a wizard who lives in Waterdeep," he explains. "Not too far from Ardeep Forest. I know him by his legendary reputation. He is the greatest practitioner of magic in this age and perhaps any other."

"So the oracle is right?" you ask. "We need to find Elminster and ask for his help?"

"I wouldn't have thought to do it," your father admits. "Elminster is a strange man, one who works by his own agenda and often ignores the wider world around him. If the oracle says he can help us, though, it has to be worth seeking him out."

You don't feel overly confident in this advice, but with nothing else to go on, what else can you possibly do?

Weeks later, you and your father find yourselves in the presence of the great wizard, a tall man with a long white beard and eyes that sparkle with wisdom. He has welcomed you into his home in the heart of Waterdeep, the most amazing city you have ever seen.

Despite what your father said about Elminster not caring much about the affairs of the wider world, the man knows about the tragedy that befell Ardeep Forest—and in far more detail than you.

"The giants have killed the rest of your family," he informs you with a grimace.

You lean into your father's embrace, and the two of you cling to each other as you absorb the confirmation of your worst fears.

"I am truly sorry for what has happened to you and your family. Unfortunately I can't change what has already come to pass, but I can teach you how to stop the giants from attacking again. It's going to take plenty of studying—for you both. Are you up for it?"

You look at your father, who nods at you to answer for both of you.

"Of course!" you say, your throat raw with grief. "Anything to put an end to their threat!"

Elminster smiles at you, clamping a hand on your shoulder, and you know right then that things are never going to be the same.

THE END

N o!" Guh says to your illusion of a ghost. "Stay away from me!"

The broken cart under Guh shatters into splinters as she tries to squirm away from the retribution of the nonexistent ghost. She's trying to flee from it, but there's no way she can move that far on her own.

"No!" you tell her. "The dead feel no remorse for you. The dead demand their revenge!"

It strikes you that you could use another spell to grease the ground beneath her so she would slide away, and you begin the preparations for it. The only question is which way should you have her go?

To one side of her, a cooking fire the size of a bonfire crackles hot and hungry. To the other, it's a short way to the lake formed by Grudd Haug damming the river. Either way would probably be bad for Guh. . . .

Toward the fire. Turn to page 36 . . .
Toward the lake. Turn to page 84 . . .

W e need to reach the oracle," you tell your father. "That way we can find out what happened to Mother and Talaren."

"Absolutely right," he says. "I just haven't been able to figure out how to get through that door." He points to the archway covered with gigantic runes.

"Ah!" Harshnag says. "This is a simple riddle, but you must be a giant to solve it. You just need to take the weapon from the statue of the type of giant you are and then touch it to the rune that matches your god."

He points to the statue of the frost giant. "That is Thrym, god of the frost giants. As a frost giant, I just need to take his weapon and touch it to the ise rune in the lower right of the arch."

"But Thrym's weapon is missing!" you point out.

"That makes the riddle a bit tougher to solve," Harshnag says with a rumbling laugh. "But not impossible." He glances about the place. "It must be around here somewhere. Just sit tight. I'll be right back."

Harshnag heads for an ice-caked door set into the chamber's southern wall, and he shatters the ice with a single blow from his ax. He disappears through the door, and soon after you hear the sounds of a terrifying battle. He returns soon after with a gigantic ax, bigger than even his own.

"Here you are!" he says. He taps the enormous ax against the ise rune, which begins to glow. The glow suffuses the mist covering the inside of the archway a moment later, and you can now see your way clear into a room beyond.

At Harshnag's urging, you and your father step through the archway and find yourself in the gigantic chamber of the oracle, standing in a massive circle of mithral-encrusted runes.

"Ask your question, and it will be answered," Harshnag says. "But you may ask only one."

Ask if your mother and brother are still alive. Turn to page 60 . . .
Ask how you can stop the giants. Turn to page 64 . . .

Oh, father!" you say. "I'm so happy I finally found you. Can't we just go home?"

As glad as he is to see you, Malaren frowns as he sets you on the ground. "I came here to see if I could learn what happened to your brother and your mother. We can't just turn back now."

"After being attacked like that by such vicious hill giants, it would be a miracle if they survived," Harshnag says to your father in a grim tone shaded with compassion. "Capture by the hill giants almost always means death."

The thought of the rest of your family being dead causes your father's shoulders to sag in defeat. For a moment, you think he's going to start sobbing, but you hope not, because if he does, there's no way for you to stop yourself from sobbing too. And you don't want to cry about the dead right now. You just want to get out of this freezing cavern and start your life over.

"I'm sorry, Father," you tell him. "I tried to save Talaren. I tried to hide away with him, just like you said to."

"It's alright, my child," he tells you as he strokes your hair. "It's not your fault. We both did the best we could."

It's at that point that you can't help but cry, and he does as well.

Once you dry your eyes, your father nods his assent at Harshnag. "It's time to set this quest aside," he says as he puts his arm around you. "I will not risk what I have found for what I have lost."

"You're wiser than I am," Harshnag says with a laugh. "But I suppose that's not a high hurdle!"

With Harshnag's help, you and your father journey to Mirabar, the largest city in the north. The frost giant takes his leave of you there.

"Farewell," he says. "May you find whatever it is you're searching for whenever you need it most!"

From Mirabar, you work your way down the appropriately named Long Road, heading toward your destroyed home. You pass through Longsaddle and Triboar, and along the way, you have many reasons to wish you could travel in the comfort of a cloud giant wizard's flying tower once again.

When you finally reach Amphail, though, your father sits you down and asks you a serious question. "I've been giving this a lot of thought," he says, "and I can't seem to make up my mind. So I'm asking for your advice.

"Our home in Ardeep Forest is no doubt destroyed. It will take years, if not decades, to rebuild it, and we'll have to do so without the assistance of your mother and brother. Should we undertake such an endeavor?"

"What choice do we have?" you ask.

Your father shrugs. "We could head for Waterdeep instead. We could set up a home there, start fresh, and not worry about being haunted by the ghosts of our past." He gazes into your eyes. "What would you like to do?"

Head for Waterdeep. Turn to page 90...
Return home. Turn to page 92...

You wave your hands and speak the proper arcane words, just as your parents taught you. When you finish, glowing missiles dart from your fingertips and bury themselves in Guh's hide. You brace yourself for her howls of pain.

With anyone else you've ever fought, a spell like this would be enough to bring them down — or at least cause them to run in the other direction. Guh, though, barely feels the magic missiles at all. Apparently her hide is too thick — or protected by too many layers of fat — for her to notice them any more than the flies buzzing around her massive bulk.

Guh's fury at your insults and your assault, though, is horrible to behold. She shrieks, all right, but in anger rather than agony. Then she begins to shudder and judder with her rage. Although she may be too heavy to launch herself at you, she can still shiver like a bowl of rancid, solidified bacon grease, and that's enough for her to shake the ramp you're standing on to pieces.

You try to leap off, but you can't find your footing. You tumble to the ground, along with the splinters of the ramp, and land hard on your back, knocking the wind out of you. Before you can recover, a vicious giant warrior leaps over and scoops you up in his hands, holding you in an iron grip. He dangles you in front of Guh and cackles in triumph.

"This runt thinks it's so smart!" Guh says as she sneers at you. "It's nothing but a baby! Throw it in with the rest of the babies! They need a new doll!"

You don't know what she's talking about, but you know it can't be good. For a moment, you think she's calling your family babies and she's going to have you tossed in with them, but you quickly realize that's not the case.

Your mother and brother shout in protest, but no one pays them any heed. The giant holding you walks out the other side of the main hall to a large pen, the kind that might be used to keep horses. Instead, there are a trio of toddler giants inside, and they squeal with glee when they see you.

The adult giant grins down at them and says, "New toy! Don't be gentle!"

That's one thing he doesn't have to worry about. Not with this group. The toddlers grab you with great enthusiasm and start fighting over you immediately. You don't last long.

THE END

You twist your hands in a horrible way, sticking your fingers down your throat. Then you remove them and point them at Guh while you recite the words to your spell.

A greenish ray springs from your hands and envelops Guh's belly and head. She roars at you in fury, and for a moment you worry that all your effort has been for nothing.

Then Guh begins to turn green at the gills. She gives you a hard look and tries to swallow down the horrible feeling rising in her throat. She fails miserably, and begins making a hiccupping noise that you know all too well.

She's too big to lean over. Instead, she just opens her mouth wide and starts to throw up.

You didn't think anything could smell worse than Guh before this, but you were wrong. Terribly, terribly wrong.

Turn to page 55...

You realize that storming into Grudd Haug would be a bad idea, so you decide to use the magic your parents taught you to disguise yourself. You would make yourself look like a giant, but you'd be an awfully short one. A few magic words and gestures later, you resemble a hobgoblin leader instead.

You step up from behind the crest of the hill overlooking Grudd Haug and stroll straight down toward it as if you own the place—or at least work there. The compound stinks even worse the closer you get to it, which you didn't think was possible.

Once you're down in the yard around the great hall, you don't have any idea where to go. You wander about for a bit, hoping that you'll find some sign of your mother and brother, but you don't spot them anywhere.

You wonder if they're in the main hall, but you're worried about going in there. As long as you're outside you have a chance to run away, but the moment you step inside a building, there's a much better chance that you'll be trapped. Especially a building where you have no idea about the layout or who you will find inside.

An ettin—a massive two-headed creature who stands a bit shorter than the hill giants—spots you and points a finger right in your face. You freeze, worried that he's figured out that you're not actually a hobgoblin.

"You!" his right head says. "Chief Guh needs another pig! Get one out of the pen and take it to her at the main hall straightaway."

You gape at the ettin for a moment, unsure of what to do. You've never handled a pig in your life, and don't particularly want to now. And as for taking it to Guh at the great hall, you don't have the slightest idea where that is.

"What are you waiting for?" the left head says with a snarl as the ettin points at a pigpen off to your right. "Hop to it! You don't want to make her mad."

He points toward the main building where you now assume Guh can be found.

Turn to page 30 . . .

You try to talk your way out of this situation. You explain that you need to find your parents and your brother—that you need to go home. The barbarians will have none of it.

Great Chief Wormblod of the Great Worm tribe of the Uthgardt barbarians has been searching for someone with magical talent to study under Retgut, the tribe's aging shaman, and you fit the bill. Your choice is to join the tribe or be cast out into the frozen wilderness to die.

You decide to study under Retgut until you see the opportunity to escape. Over time, though, you come to appreciate the Uthgardt way of life, and when Retgut dies, you ascend to become the tribe's young shaman. Unwilling to leave your new people without a shaman, you set out to find someone to replace you.

Uthgar willing, it'll happen soon.

THE END

Harshnag claps you on the back and walks with you up a set of stairs that terminates in a thirty-foot-tall set of double doors covered with images of giants fighting dragons. You reach up to touch their glittering surface, and you realize that they're covered with ice. You push on them, but they don't budge.

"Step aside, little one," Harshnag says. You do as you are told, and he charges up and smashes his shoulder into the doors. The ice on them shatters, and they slam inward before his incredible might.

You follow the frost giant into the cavernous chamber beyond. Every surface inside the room is rimed with ice, including seven gigantic statues. The first and largest of these—a robed giant with its face hidden beneath a deep-hooded cowl—stands in the center of the room.

The other statues kneel in two rows, to the central statue's left and right. Again, they feature each of the giant types: hill, stone, frost, fire, cloud, and storm. Each of the smaller statues faces the one in the center, and all except for the frost giant statue offer their weapons up to the main statue.

The main statue gazes at an archway, and arranged around the arch are six runes you do not recognize, each engraved with a silvery metal called mithral. The archway is blocked by a stone wall covered by a thick, swirling mist.

You're not as concerned with the statues or the arch, however, as you are with the other person you see in the room: an elf dressed in tattered robes. It's your father!

You shout in delight and race over for him to draw you up into a warm embrace.

"My child!" he says, tears of relief running down his face. "I thought you were dead!"

Try to solve the riddle of the runes. Turn to page 69...
Ask your father to bring you home. Turn to page 71...

You cast your spell next to Guh rather than directly at her, creating a slippery patch on the floor between her and the wall. She turns to see what you've done and the movement edges her bulk onto the patch, causing her to slip just as you planned.

The giant yelps in terror as she begins to slide in the direction of the wall, groping for some way to stop herself. Unfortunately for her, she's covered with so much grease from the food she eats and the fact that she never washes that she can't possibly find purchase on anything, no matter how much she flails about.

Guh slams into the wall of the main hall with all of her tremendous bulk, and it gives way as if she were a brick tearing through paper. She loses little of her momentum as she smashes through it, and from there she slides straight outside into the bare sunlight and into the lake beyond.

"Help me, you idiots!" she screams as her followers gawk at her. "I can't swim!"

An oil slick forms on the water around her, splashing up a wall of foul water. She screeches as if the water burns her, and this finally breaks her followers out of their shock. They burst into action, chasing after her.

A number of hill giants race out to the lake's edge to try to save her, but they can't get a grip on her greasy, formless flesh. It's like trying to grab hold of rancid butter.

Guh slides farther and farther into the water, screaming louder as she goes. The rest of the giants in the hall also emerge into the light and try to help the others save her. Despite the many hands struggling to grab Guh, the rescue effort is hopeless.

You don't stick around to witness Guh's struggles and her ultimate fate. Instead, you run back down her feeding ramp and make a beeline for the cage holding your mother and brother.

The goblins guarding the cage see that you're ready for a fight, and they don't try to stop you. Instead, they decide this is the perfect time to quit their awful jobs, and they abandon their posts and head for the hills. This leaves you alone with your mother and brother, still trapped in the cage.

"Over there!" Your mother points to a set of keys hanging from a nail in a nearby wall, and you retrieve them and unlock the cage. They're free!

They come tumbling out of the cage and give you a quick hug to the echoes of Guh's distant screams. That's all you have time for at the moment.

Turn to page 93...

You aren't about to go lock yourself in a cage. Not if you can do anything to avoid it. You just need a little time to ready a spell.

"You're fat and useless," you say to Guh as you begin. "How do you manage to get anyone here to help you?"

Every bit of chatter in the room ceases at that moment. None of the hill giants, goblins, and hobgoblins can believe that anyone would talk to Guh that way—much less someone as small as you. None of them has ever been so brave, despite how poorly she's treated them all.

Guh herself seems struck dumb by your audacity. She opens her mouth to speak to you, but she's so shocked at your insult that she can't squeak out an intelligible response.

"I notice there are only male giants here," you say to her. "Did you have all the female giants killed or run off? Or did they leave on their own because they could no longer stomach how disgusting you are?"

As she gapes at you in shock, you work your spell faster. You realize that sooner or later she's going to come to her senses enough to order her underlings to murder you. Or maybe she'll just throw you straight down her gigantic gullet. You need to be ready to attack when that happens. You're not sure it's going to do you any good, but you refuse to go down without a fight.

"That would explain why there aren't any of them within smelling distance, at least," you continue. "Does everyone who works here have to plug their noses with wax to get near you, or do they all stink as badly as you do?"

"You nasty little beast!" Guh finally says. "No one talks to me like that! Ever! I'm on the verge of becoming the largest giant that ever lived! When that happens, the gods themselves will have to bow before my spectacular self, and the hill giants will be the biggest bosses in the entire land!"

"That is possibly the stupidest plan I've ever heard," you tell her. "And I have a little brother. You would not believe the silly things he says. But even he wouldn't come up with something as ridiculous as that."

You size her up. "And what's that gotten you? You have more fat on you than an entire herd of cows. The only thing you can hope for now is that death will take you before you suffer too much from your gluttony."

Guh's face grows beet red, and she looks as if she's about to explode. You hope that maybe she'll keel over from a heart attack before she can respond, but you're not so lucky.

She points a fat finger at you and screams, "Kill this one! Better yet, make this beast into a sandwich, and I'll eat it to death!"

You finally have your spell ready. Time to use it.

Fire magic missiles! Turn to page 75 . . .
Shine a ray of sickness! Turn to page 77 . . .

Harshnag draws his battle-ax as he stares up into the sky. You follow his line of sight to spy something soaring down out of the freezing clouds toward you. At first you think it must be some kind of eagle, or perhaps a giant bat, but it grows larger by the second. You soon realize that it's a gigantic blue dragon, and it's coming straight at you!

"I don't know why this creature is coming here now," Harshnag says. "But I cannot permit such an evil beast to foul this sacred ground. You should flee as fast as your feet will carry you! I will stay here to defend the Eye of the All-Father and to ensure your safe passage!"

The dragon screams down toward the giant, lightning arcing out of its mouth to strike Harshnag's readied ax. The frost giant roars in pain as steam leaps from his scorched limbs, but he does not stagger even one step back.

Your father takes you by the hand. "We should help him," he says uncertainly. "But if we do, we might never find your mother and brother." He stands there paralyzed, unable to decide what to do.

It's up to you.

Fight the dragon! Turn to page 95 . . .
Run! Turn to page 98 . . .
Talk with the dragon. Turn to page 108 . . .

After giving the choice some thought, you speak. "I can't bear the idea of seeing our home in ruins," you say. "It would be like losing Mother and Talaren all over again."

Your father nods in understanding. "Waterdeep it is, then," he says as he gives you a hug.

Many days later, you reach the City of Splendors and walk through its gates for the first time. Your father has been here many times before, it turns out. He reveals to you that long before you were born, he and your mother were adventurers.

"We gave all that up when your mother became pregnant with you," he tells you over dinner one night in your new home in the North Ward, a quiet section of town where noble families live alongside those who have money left over from their adventuring days, like your father. "Being a parent isn't suited to a life of exploration and looting, I'm afraid."

"Will you teach me how to be a great adventurer?" you ask him.

He gets a funny look on his face, some mixture of suspicion and pride. "Why in the world would you want to take up a life like that?"

"You make it sound so intriguing," you say.

You don't tell him the truth, although you suppose he could guess at it. Someday, when you know enough magic and have enough know-how, you promise yourself you're going to track down the giants who destroyed your home—who took your mother and your brother—and you're going to make sure they can never do anything like that to anyone else ever again.

"I suppose it might seem like that," he says with an uncertain laugh. "But I'm sure you'd find out the hard way just how wrong you are."

THE END

W e have to go home," you tell your father. "There's no other way."

"Of course," he says with grim certainty. "Thanks for keeping me on the right path."

As you reach the ruins of your home days later, though, you're not so sure you made the right choice. You admit to yourself that you harbored in your heart the ridiculous hope that you might come back to find your mother and brother there, already cleaning the place up. Instead, you find nothing but evidence that scavengers following in the giants' wake have picked it over. No one else has been here since.

"Don't worry," your father tells you as you set up camp where your proud tower-tree once stood. "There's nothing in this world that can't be rebuilt." His voice cracks as he puts an arm around you. "No matter how long it takes."

THE END

You lead your mother and brother out of the hall and race over to a pen where the giants have been keeping all sorts of animals to feed to Guh—including a couple of horses. They're clearly tame, but you don't care to wonder what happened to their riders. You break them out of the pen and the three of you mount up, your mother on one horse and your brother sitting in front of you on the other.

You set your heels to the horses and race out of Grudd Haug, leaving it far behind as fast as you can. In the darkness behind you, you can hear the giants still struggling to retrieve Guh from the lake, and you can't help but think she's getting what she deserves.

"Thank you!" your mother says as she brings her horse to gallop alongside yours. "My little one has grown up to be quite the hero!"

Much as you miss your father—who you later learn has died in the far north—you can't help but smile at that.

THE END

W e can't abandon Harshnag!" you say to your father. "If not for his help, I never would have found you in the first place!"

Malaren reaches down to tousle your hair, happy to see you making the right decision. "Exactly right," he tells you. "We can't leave such a good friend in the moment of his greatest need, can we?"

You've never been so proud of your father as you are at that moment. You know that standing up to a dragon might mean the death of all of you, but you can't bear the thought of abandoning such a true friend—and you're glad to know he feels the same way. You take your father's hand, and turn with him to rush up behind Harshnag and help him take on the dragon.

It's at that moment that you fully realize what you've gotten yourself into. The dragon is at least as large as Harshnag, maybe larger. It's hard to tell when the beast is wrapping itself around the frost giant and gnawing on his forearm with teeth as long and sharp as swords.

In a battle between such gargantuan creatures, it's hard to see what kind of help you can offer. You feel foolish for having suggested that you might have any influence at all. You turn to your father to apologize, but you see he has set his jaw in a way that you recognize all too well. He's not about to back down from this fight, no matter how desperate it might be.

Your father steps between you and the dragon and begins to prepare a spell. Soon enough, he has it ready to go, but he still hasn't cast it. You watch him uncertainly, unsure of what he is waiting for.

"What's wrong?" you ask. "You need to help Harshnag! The dragon will kill him!"

"I know," he says, exasperated. He moves back and forth, trying to find the right angle for his attack. "I don't want to hurt Harshnag too!" he says.

You decide to help out in the only way you can. You're not a powerful enough wizard to hurt the dragon, but that doesn't mean you're useless in a fight. Not even this one.

You sprint off to the right, screaming and yelling at the top of your lungs. On top of that, you wave your arms to make sure no one could possibly ignore you. "Hey, you icy old worm! Bet you can't catch me!"

The dragon roars as it cranes its neck to see who dares to taunt it so brazenly in the middle of a fight. It spies you standing there waving your arms wildly at it, and it opens its massive maw so that it can fire a bolt of lightning at you.

You freeze, certain that you've made a fatal mistake. While Harshnag might be able to shrug off the effects of a dragon's lightning bolt, you're pretty sure that a naked blast of such raw energy will fry you to a blackened crisp.

Your father tosses something at the creature at that moment, though. It lands behind the dragon and explodes into a gigantic ball of fire. The blast tears into the dragon and sets it ablaze, but it also knocks both it and Harshnag off their feet. The two of them tumble toward you, and your father screams at you to move.

You turn and sprint away from the towering creatures as they topple toward you. You pump your legs as fast and hard as you can, but the shadow the creatures cast envelops you as you go. You want to give up and rest your aching chest and your tired limbs, but you don't dare. To hesitate for even half a step means guaranteeing you'll be crushed to death.

You feel a great rush of wind as the creatures begin to crumple behind you, and you dive forward at the last instant. You can feel the tip of the dragon's snout brush against your boots, but it just misses you.

The shock wave from the humongous landing, though, hurls you into a nearby snowbank. As you crawl out of it, your father shouts at you. "Run! Run, and don't look back!"

Flee! Turn to page 116 . . .
Face the dragon! Turn to page 105 . . .

Harshnag can handle himself!" you tell your father as you grab his hand. "We need to leave!"

Your father doesn't try to argue with you. Instead, he sprints ahead, dragging you along by the hand. "Where are we going?" he shouts.

"I don't know!" you say. "Away from here!"

"That I can do," he says. He charges forward at top speed, urging you to move faster than you ever have before.

You put every bit of energy you have into keeping up with your father, but his legs are longer than yours and you just can't match his speed. Despite that, he refuses to let go of you—not until the dragon swoops down in front of you, cutting off your path.

"Where do you think you're going?" the dragon asks as she lands hard on the ice, which cracks beneath her claws.

Despite yourself, you scream in terror. Your father lets go of your hand and places himself between the dragon and you. You appreciate the gesture, even though you know the dragon could tear through your father with a single swipe of her claws.

"We don't have any issue with you," he tells her. "Let us leave in peace!"

"The time for that is past, I'm afraid," she says. "You were with that giant, and he hurt me. You meant something to him, so it's time for you to die." She rears back her head to launch a bolt of lightning.

Before she can loose the electricity, though, Harshnag's gigantic ax comes whirling through the air overhead and punches the creature in the chest. She reels backward, howling in pain.

"Run!" your father says to you as he prepares a spell to use against the dragon. "No time to argue about it! Get clear!"

You listen to your father and flee back the way you came. You nearly run into Harshnag, who scoops you up in his hands.

"Put me down!" you shout at him. "We need to get away from the dragon!"

"Well, *you* do for sure," the frost giant says without missing a single step. "And for that, I think I have just the solution. Can you fly?"

"What? No!" you say, confused. "Of course not."

"Then tuck and roll!"

Before you can ask him what he means by that, he hurls you up in the air, out over the entrance to the Eye of the All-Father. You scream the entire way, certain that Harshnag has thrown you to your death.

Turn to page 102 . . .

You can't see this ending well. As your father and Harshnag creep up behind the dragon, you spin on your heels and flee.

"Huh?" the dragon says as her laughter trails off. "Where are you going? We were having so much fun!"

It's then that your father hurls a fireball at the monster. It soars toward the beast, blazing like a miniature sun the entire way, and then it explodes.

It goes off right underneath the dragon, scorching her belly and blasting her into the air. The creature howls in pain and surprise, but manages to land on her feet despite this, and she spins about. She raises her head once again, surprisingly ready for when Harshnag levels a devastating ax swing at her exposed neck. Meanwhile, your father is already preparing another spell, just in case Harshnag's effort falls short.

You stop in your tracks to watch the battle play out. For a wild moment, hope leaps in your heart, and you start to imagine that you, your father, and Harshnag might not just survive the day, but may even actually triumph!

Before the giant's blow can strike true, the dragon unleashes a blast of lightning from her mouth. You comfort yourself with the thought that even if it stops the giant, your father should be able to get off another spell against the dragon before she can turn her attention back to you.

Before your stunned eyes, though, the lightning actually forks as it leaves the dragon's mouth. One branch strikes Harshnag's ax, knocking it from his hand. The other one lances straight through your father, who falls over, a smoldering wreck.

The dragon launches herself at the stunned frost giant then, laying into him tooth and nail. It's not long before the dragon finishes him off, leaving him cooling there on the ice-covered ground.

The dragon then turns her attention to you. She charges after you and catches you in her claws.

"You're an entertaining one," the dragon says to you. "And relatively harmless. Not like those others. What would you say to becoming my pet?"

You don't see that you have a choice. "What are my duties?" you ask.

"Once a day," the dragon says, "you need to make me laugh. Keep that up, and you'll live comfortably in my lair. Otherwise . . . "

You resign yourself to your fate. "Something tells me you're a tough audience," you say with a deep sigh.

THE END

Realizing what Harshnag meant, you tuck yourself into a ball before you come soaring down out of the air to crash into a massive snowbank. Fortunately, the snow is soft and cushions your landing. At least you're away from the dragon, although it takes you what seems like forever to climb out of the snow.

As you emerge, you find a floating ship hovering over the hole you made when you landed. It looks like a large sled held aloft by a huge red balloon. A rope ladder tumbles down from the edge of it, and a man in black leather armor and a matching mask calls to you.

"We're with the Cult of the Dragon," he says. A roar from the blue dragon sounds in the distance, and he shakes his head. "A different dragon! Not that one! We're here to save you!"

Board the ship. Turn to page 118...
Refuse their offer. Turn to page 121...

"I don't see what's so funny about my mother and brother being captured by giants!" you say defiantly to the laughing dragon.

"That's priceless!" the dragon says. "They get kidnapped by a bunch of massive idiots, and you come all the way up here to figure that out?"

"That's not funny!"

"Of course not!" the dragon says. "Not to you! You had to trek all the way up here through the cold and on your feet. But to me? It's hilarious!"

As the dragon laughs, you see your father and Harshnag moving into position to attack again. She has let her guard down at this point and is as vulnerable as she's ever going to be.

Still, she's an ancient dragon! As large as Harshnag is and as powerful as your father might be, do they really have a prayer against her?

Run! Turn to page 100 . . .
Attack the dragon! Turn to page 110 . . .

Y ou're not about to abandon your father when you have only just found him. As far as you know, he could be the only family you have left.

"No!" you tell your father. "I won't leave you!"

He sighs in a mixture of exasperation and pride. "You're too brave for your own good!" he shouts over at you.

The dragon rears back then, pushing herself up on her spindly arms to glare down at you. Her teeth flash with barely controlled lightning that crackles along them from one side of her mouth to the other, and you feel the hairs on the back of your neck start to rise.

"You dare stand between me and the oracle?" the dragon says with a vicious snarl. "The penalty for that is a swift and painful death!"

The dragon opens her mouth, but before she can release the lightning, Harshnag reaches up and punches her across her scaly snout. She roars in pain and bites down on the giant, catching Harshnag's neck in her mouth.

The giant roars back at the monster in both agony and determination. He shoves the handle of his ax into the dragon's mouth, keeping her from biting down any further. Then he hauls on the business end of the ax and levers the teeth apart so he can work his way free.

The dragon isn't one to be put off by such a show of strength, though. As Harshnag pushes her away, she unleashes another bolt of lightning from her mouth. This catches the giant straight through his skull, causing his eyes, nose, and mouth to glow with electricity.

Harshnag tumbles backward, his head smoking from absorbing the massive charge. He growls no more as the dragon shoves herself off of him and turns her attention to your father.

He already has another spell ready. He rubs something between his fingers that glows softly in the encroaching darkness and then flings his arms wide. A sheath of living fire envelops him from head to toe, and he shouts up at the dragon, "You will leave us alone!"

"Hardly," the dragon says with a low snicker. She launches herself at him and knocks him flying with a single swipe of her vicious claws.

Just like that, your father is gone, and you're all alone against the dragon.

You refuse to run—mostly because you're sure that you wouldn't have a chance. The dragon's just too fast, and you have nowhere to go anyhow. Especially now that both Harshnag and your father are gone. There's one thing you want to know, though.

"Why?" you ask the dragon.

She laughs as she creeps toward you and glares down through heavy-lidded eyes. "Because I am the great and powerful Iymrith," she says. "And I do not let anyone get between me and what I want. Those who try shall pay with their lives."

The last thing you see is a flash of electricity.

THE END

W ait!" you shout as you step out from behind your father, hoping to come up with a solution that doesn't involve you all being killed. "Can't we talk about this?"

The dragon knocks Harshnag aside with a swing of her mighty tail, and the great warrior stumbles to his knees. Rather than leaping to his feet and charging back into the fight, though, the giant freezes there, still on the ground, waiting to see how the creature responds to your question.

"Can we?" the dragon says as she spins toward you and eyes you with suspicion. "Personally, I love a good chat, but most times when I indulge myself in such, I discover that the people I'm talking with only wish me harm."

Your father responds to that with indignation. "We wish you no ill. We just want to be—"

"Silence!" the dragon roars, lightning tracing through her teeth and crackling around her jaws. "I was speaking with the young one. Creatures like you and the giant are too old. The world has already sunk its claws into you—filled you with its prejudices—and you cannot be trusted!"

Your father staggers back a couple steps, cowed by the dragon's ferocious response, the color draining from his face. Once he regains his composure, he backs away another step and swings his arms wide to gesture for you to talk. You nod at him and take a deep breath before you begin.

"We came here to speak to the oracle," you tell the dragon. "Hill giants attacked our home many miles from here, and my mother and brother went missing. We came here to ask about their fate."

The dragon peers down at you as if this is the most ridiculous thing she's ever heard come out of anyone's mouth. "And what, exactly, did the oracle tell you?"

You swallow hard. You don't see any reason to lie about this. "It said that my mother and brother were captured by the hill giant chief Guh and taken to a place called Grudd Haug. It's many miles from here. Farther south than even our home."

The dragon seems to contemplate this for a moment. Then she begins to shudder, and you wonder what you could have said that might have terrified a dragon into shivering like that.

Then the great beast snorts out loud, and lightning cracks from her nostrils. She chortles as if the electricity tickles.

You realize then that the dragon isn't scared at all—certainly not of anything you said. Instead, she bursts out laughing about your family's fate.

Turn to page 103...

It's not funny!" you shout at the dragon as you march toward her.

The dragon thinks this is even funnier than before. "And now you think you can take on me, the mighty Iymrith? Ha!" She leans down to laugh in your face.

You don't know a lot of magic yet, but you have one spell you think might help in this situation. You reach into your pouch and produce a bit of glowing moss that your mother gave you, and you recite the magic words. Then you march straight into the dragon's laughter and smack the moss onto the end of her snout.

As the dragon's nose erupts into a blazing ball of glowing light, she stops laughing.

"You foolish elf!" she shouts at you in surprise. "That didn't hurt at all!"

You scramble backward as fast as you can. "I wasn't trying to hurt you," you tell the dragon. "Not directly."

"I can't see!" the dragon says as she tries to peer past the light at the end of her nose.

It's your turn to laugh — or you would if you weren't terrified that the dragon is going to chase you and kill you for your little trick. Fortunately, your father and Harshnag leap forward to attack her before she can work out how to see around the light to get at you.

Your father offers up a wordless shout as he charges the beast, no doubt hoping to draw her away from you. In return, the dragon knocks your father aside with a blind sweep of a claw, and he goes spinning into a distant snowbank. Harshnag, meanwhile, levels his battle-ax at the creature and brings it down on her exposed neck.

The dragon howls in pain and rage, but the frost giant's blow has knocked the fight out of her. Harshnag chops at her again and again until she falls still.

Turn to page 119 . . .

You wait until the sun sets, and then you sneak down toward the main hall of Grudd Haug under the cover of darkness. The area is filled with goblins, hobgoblins, and worse, along with several hill giants—all male. You don't find any sign of your mother and brother, so you sneak over to the hall and peer through a window.

Inside, you see even more goblins, hobgoblins, and giants—including one even more massive than the rest. This is the only female hill giant around, but she's humongous, much bigger than the males. She's so fat, her legs have nearly disappeared beneath her, and you wonder if there's any way she can move on her own at all.

As you watch, a goblin literally shovels food into her rotting mouth. She seems as if she might never stop eating.

Turn to page 34…

You're grief stricken to be forced to leave your father and Harshnag behind, even though you know that's exactly what they would have wanted you to do. You agree to let the airship carry you away, and you don't scream about it at all for fear that this might bring Iymrith after you.

Later, as the airship leaves the Eye of the All-Father behind, you spy a dragon shape rising from the snow-capped peaks above it to roar into the sky. You know then that your father and Harshnag must be dead. You made the right choice, no matter how hard it may have been.

Many days later, the airship arrives over Ardeep Forest, and you lead it to the place where your home once stood. Seeing the forest from the sky makes you realize just how complete the destruction is.

"These were hill giants?" the cult leader asks.

You affirm this with a nod as the man accompanies you to the ground.

"They were part of Chief Guh's tribe, and they hailed from Grudd Haug," you tell him.

He puts a hand on your shoulder to comfort you. "I will report this back to our lord, Klauth. With luck, he will take revenge on them for you soon."

You don't believe that will ever happen, but you thank the man just the same.

As the airship disappears into the sky, you hear a voice behind you and turn to see your brother emerging from the ruins of your home.

"Talaren!" you cry as you wrap him in a tight hug you never want to let end.

"Mother's gone," he says. "She died saving me. I raced all the way home to find it gone."

"Same with father," you tell him. "There's just us now. We're all that's left."

He continues to hug you. "I suppose that will have to be enough."

THE END

As much as you want to stay and help your father and Harshnag take down the dragon, you know that this is far beyond your meager abilities. On top of that, the dragon clearly has them outmatched. If you were to stand with them, you would die for sure.

So despite wanting to stay with your father, you do as he orders. You turn tail and run, sprinting away from him as fast as your legs will carry you.

The only problem is that you don't really know where to go, other than away from the dragon. The Eye of the All-Father sits at the end of a long and complicated set of passages, and although you tried, you weren't able to keep track of all the twists and turns as Harshnag led you through them. The best you can do is run away as fast as you can and hope that you somehow wind up running in a safe direction.

Unfortunately, hope makes for a poor plan.

Despite that, you have no other choice at this point, so you give it your best try. You run until you're out of breath—until the icy air feels like it's stabbing you in the lungs—and you collapse into a nearby snowbank, hoping to find some temporary respite. You rest there for a moment, wondering if you could possibly have gone far enough to evade the dragon yet.

As you work to catch your wind, you try to figure out where you are. Unfortunately, you have no clue. All you see are winding passages formed from snow and ice, and you can't even tell which way the sun hangs in the sky. Any way out of the area seems as good as another.

A distant roar echoes through the passageways and reminds you that the battle with the dragon isn't over. Once the mighty beast finishes with Harshnag and possibly your father, she's bound to come chasing after you, and you can't possibly outrace her. You need to find shelter from the beast—if there is such a thing—and soon. And you're not going to be able to manage that while you're sitting in a snowbank.

You start moving again, hunting for a solution to your dilemma. Soon you come to a cliff overlooking a long slope of ice that descends into darkness. You peer over the edge, unable to see where the slope might end, but you don't see a clear alternative either—at least not one that doesn't lead straight back into what sounds like a losing battle against the dragon.

You grit your teeth and decide to give the slope a shot. You lower yourself over the edge and try to crawl down as carefully as you can. You don't get too far, though, before one of your handholds crumbles beneath your fingers. You struggle to hang on with your other hand for a long moment, but the handhold there gives way.

You slide down into the darkness, unable to stop yourself and gaining speed with every second.

Turn to page 35...

As insane as it might be, the airship full of dragon cultists seems like the safer bet. You leap for the rope ladder and scramble up to the top. When you get there, the cultists welcome you aboard.

"We've been following the blue dragon, Iymrith, for ages," their leader explains. "She's been investigating the resurgence of giant tribes around the Sword Coast, and our dragon-god, Klauth, wants to know more about it himself."

"Hill giants attacked my home in Ardeep Forest!" you tell them. You notice that the other cultists are getting the ship under way. "Wait! Where are we going? My father's still down there fighting that dragon!"

"Then I'm afraid he is lost," the leader says to you. "To let Iymrith see us would be to court death. We must leave immediately—but we would be happy to take you home to see what the giants have done."

Turn to page 114 . . .

You race over to where your father fell and dig him out from the snowbank. He's unconscious but breathing—just barely. You sigh with relief and hold him to you until the giant gently nudges you aside.

Harshnag picks your father up and clucks his tongue at him. "You should know better than to take on a dragon like that, little one," he says.

The giant looks down at you. "We should bring him to a city where he can recover. How does Neverwinter sound to you?"

You repeat the city's name and let it roll on your tongue. Going there means giving up on your mother and brother, but in your heart you know they're already dead.

"It sounds much warmer than here," you say with a chuckle. You reach up to take the giant's spare hand. "Thank you so much."

The frost giant actually blushes. "I couldn't have defeated the dragon without your help. Good people need to stick together," he says. "And stick up for one another. No matter their size."

THE END

After the time you've had, leaping into an airship full of dragon-worshipping cultists so you can avoid the wrath of a dragon is just too much. "Forget it!" you shout up at the airship. "I'll try my luck on my own!"

"Suit yourself," the leader shouts down. At a signal from him, the cultists roll up their ladder and float away. You wonder if you should check to see who won the battle: your father and Harshnag or the dragon. Then you hear a mighty roar that answers your question in the worst possible way.

You dive back into the snowbank from whence you came, and you remain hidden there for several minutes, shivering from more than the cold. Eventually you spy the blue dragon as she flaps her way back into the sky. She ignores you entirely and wings off toward the east, heading to a destination you'll never know.

You climb back out of the snow and realize you're entirely on your own. Your father and Harshnag are dead, and the airship has long since gone. There's nothing for you to do but venture back into the wilderness—this time on your own.

You manage to climb down out of the mountains and try to limp toward Mirabar, the last city where you stocked up on goods before Harshnag led you into the Spine of the World. You somehow overshoot it, though, and wind up too far west. Rather than double back, you decide to keep going.

Colder and thinner than you were in the mountains, you eventually find the Blackford Road and make your way to Luskan, the northernmost city on the Sword Coast. You head immediately for the docks, searching for a ship on which you can work for your passage.

"Where are you headed?" asks the Chultan captain of a ship called *The Mistcliff Runner*.

"Anywhere," you tell him. "As long as it's warm."

"You don't have a port to call home?" he says with a warm chuckle.

"Not anymore," you tell him. "The only thing I want is to never be cold again!"

THE END

The images in this book were created by Alessandra Pisano, Amir Salehi, Chris Seaman, Conceptopolis, Cory Trego-Erdner, Daren Bader, Dave Dorman, Emi Kuioka, Emily Fiegenschuh, Eric Belisle, Eric Deschamps, Hector Ortiz, John-Paul Balmet, Jon Hodgson, Julian Kok Joon Wen, Justin Sweet, Kate Irwin, Lars Grant-West, Lee Moyer, Mark Behm, Mark Molnar, Olga Drebas, Randy Gallegos, Scott M. Fischer, Sidharth Chaturvedi, Steve Prescott, Thom Tenery, Tyler Jacobson, and Wayne England.

The cover illustrations were created by Justin Sweet and Scott M. Fischer.

CANDLEWICK
ENTERTAINMENT

Copyright © 2018 by Wizards of the Coast LLC
Written by Matt Forbeck
Designed by Crazy Monkey Creative and Rosie Bellwood
Edited by Kirsty Walters
Published in the U.K. 2018 by Studio Press,
part of the Bonnier Publishing Group.
All rights reserved.

First U.S. edition 2018
Library of Congress Catalog Card Number pending
ISBN 978-1-5362-0245-8 (hardcover) 978-1-5362-0244-1 (paperback)
18 19 20 21 22 23 WKT 10 9 8 7 6 5 4 3 2 1
Printed in Shenzhen, Guangdong, China
Candlewick Press, 99 Dover Street, Somerville, Massachusetts 02144
visit us at www.candlewick.com

Don't miss the other Dungeons & Dragons® Endless Quest® titles!

Escape the Underdark
Into the Jungle
To Catch a Thief

Or these Dungeons & Dragons titles available from Candlewick Press:

Monsters and Heroes of the Realms
Dungeonology